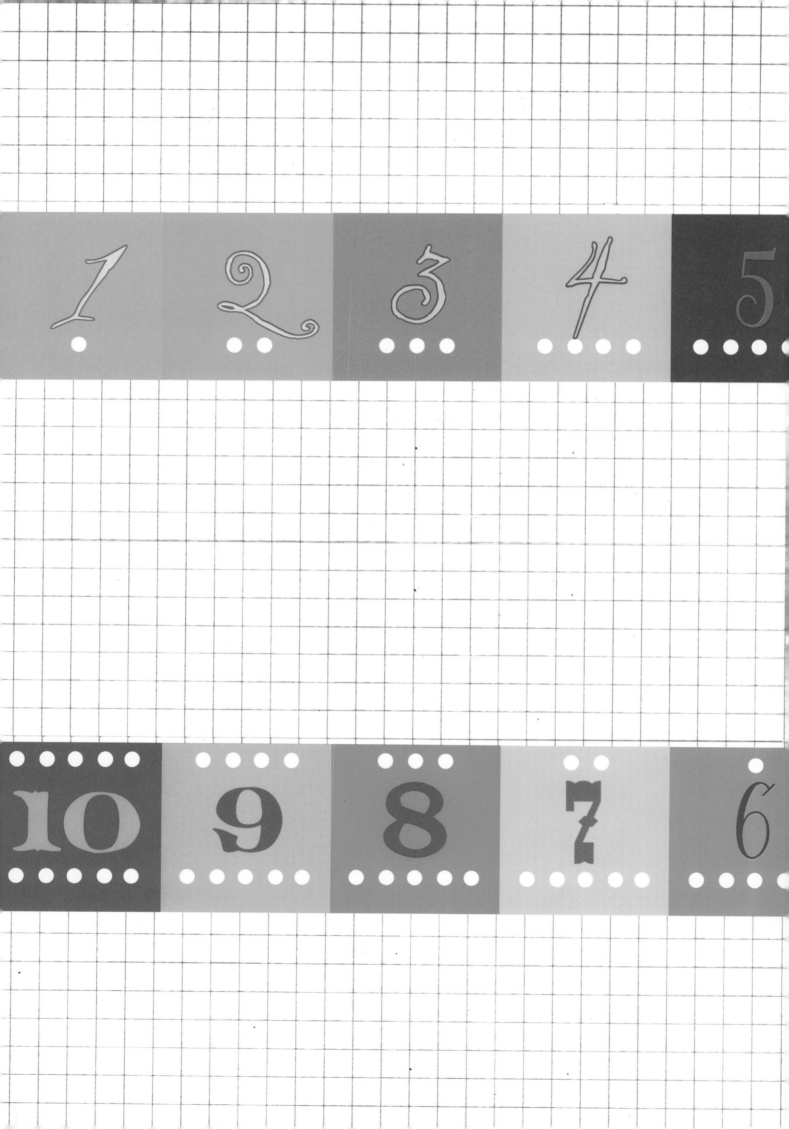

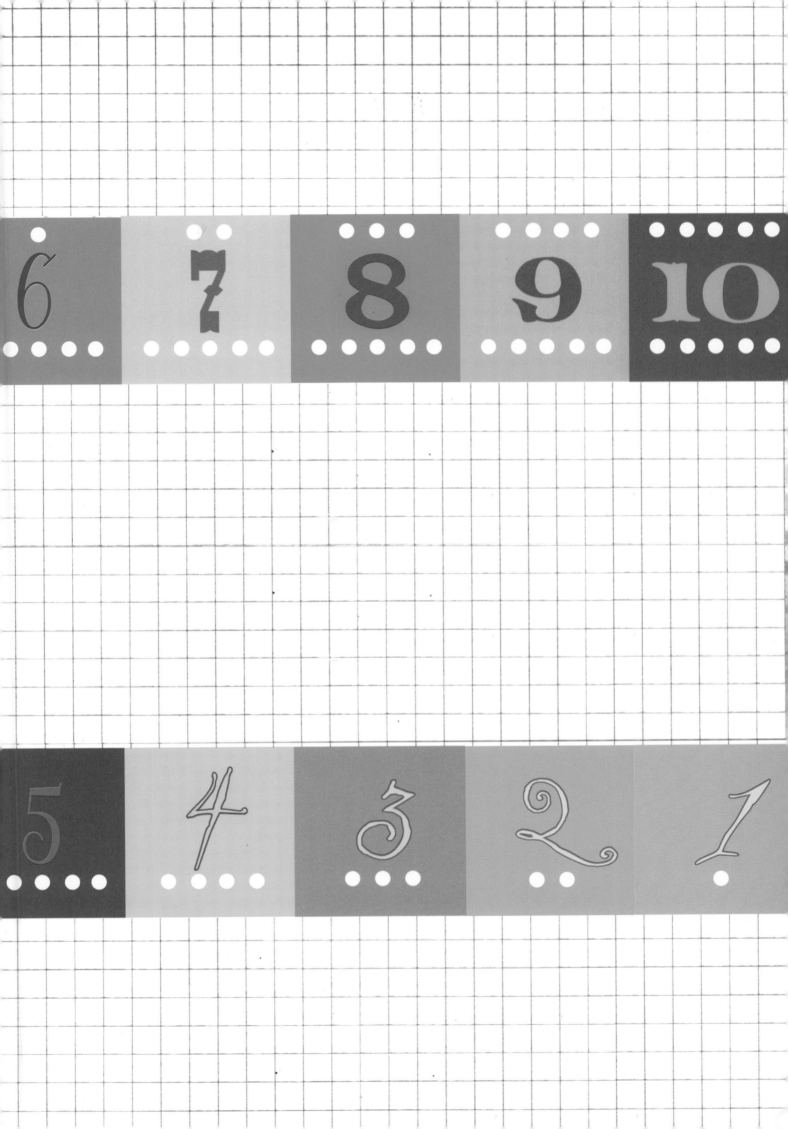

The Numbers Dance

A Counting Comedy

josephine nobisso

illustrated by dasha ziborova

GINGERBREAD HOUSE
westhampton beach, new york

And-a-1
And-a-2
And-a-3
And-a-4
Four dainty numbers waltz across a floor.

1 spins—elegant, straight and true.
2 tiptoes from shoe to shoe.
3 swirls 'round, so curvy and plump
With 4 on one leg, glide and jump!

Here come swinging 5 and 6
Who are always getting in a fix!
They samba and conga and
Rumba 'cross the floor!
The others want to leave now,
Scrambling for the door.

1 gets bumped.
2 gets dumped.
3 gets slumped
On 4 who's crumped.

5 and 6 help them off the floor.
Now all of the numbers go dancing like before.

And-a-1
And-a-2
And-a-3
And-a-4
Four go fluttering, flying 'cross the floor.

5 and 6 jitter and jive,
Changing places, 6 and 5!

They can't believe what happens then:
Enter 7, 8, 9, and 10!
Leaping and hoofing and tramping, these prance,
Kicking up heels in a wild Line Dance!

7 in a boot, stamps her stump.
8 twirls a hat upon his rump.
9 wraps scarves around her lump.
And 10 gallops hard, fa-rump, ga-zump.
They're clodding on the dance floor:
CLUMP, CLUMP, CLUMP!

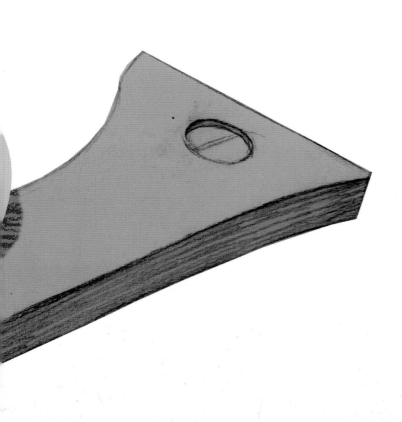

1 gets knocked.
2 gets socked.
3 gets blocked
With 4 who's rocked.

Even 5 and 6 feel shock,
Finding themselves in a strange head-lock.

1, 2, 3, 4, 5, and 6
Lying in a heap like pick-up-sticks!

7 and 8 and 9 and 10
Never even notice; they're at it again:
7 hops up, taking the lead.
8 flings a hat like a bucking steed.
9 cartwheels on a tumbleweed.
But 10's been trampled in the dance stampede.

7 and 8 and 9 still go—
"Swing your partner! Do-si-do!"
7 leaps up, flicking her spur.
8 barks out, "Yessir! Yessir!"
But 9 gets snagged on a cocklebur.

7 and 8 shout out, "Yahoo!"
Then find themselves in a tight lasso
With 9 and 10, who've been rustled, too.

1
2
3
4
5
6
7
8
9
10

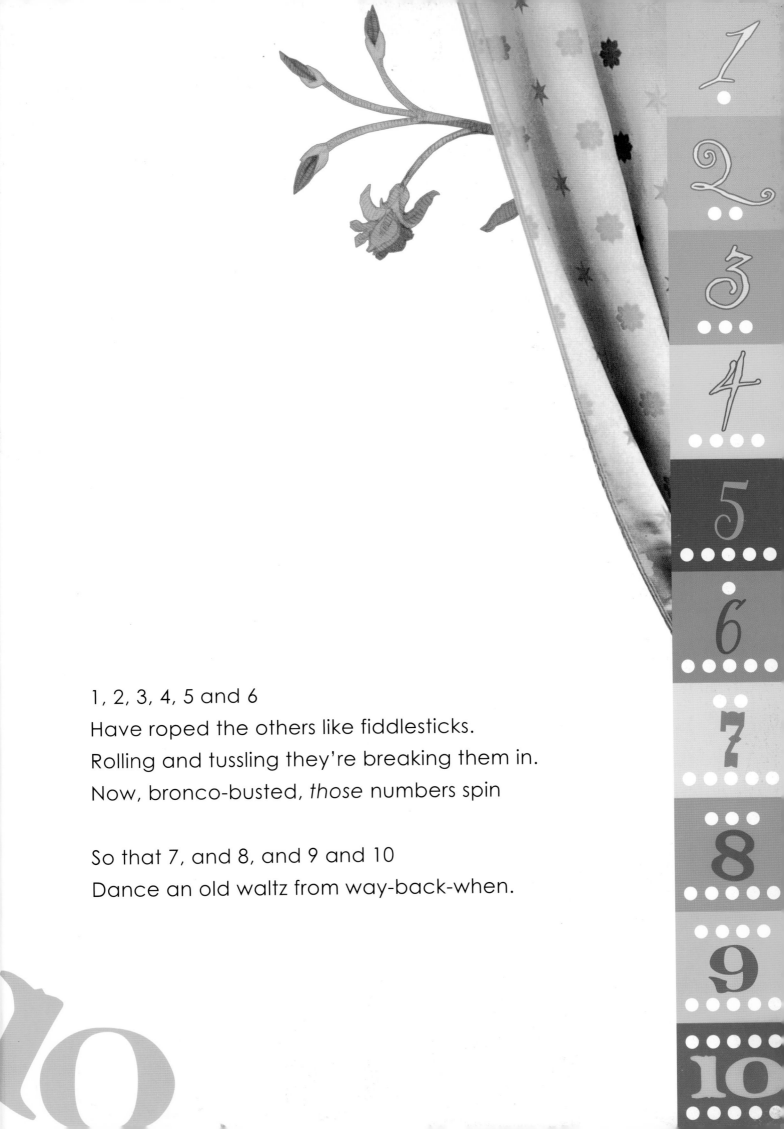

1, 2, 3, 4, 5 and 6
Have roped the others like fiddlesticks.
Rolling and tussling they're breaking them in.
Now, bronco-busted, *those* numbers spin

So that 7, and 8, and 9 and 10
Dance an old waltz from way-back-when.

And-a-1

And-a-2

And-a-3

And-a-4

Curtsy and bow like they did before.

5 and 6 waltz for a while,
Then give each other a knowing smile.
They dip and bow and pivot and hug
Then both break out in a jitterbug!
They shimmy and boogie and twist and reel
Showing all the others just how they feel.

Then-a-1
And-a-2
And-a-3
And-a-4
And-a-5
And-a-6
And-a-7
And-a-8
And-a-9
And-a-10
Dance their OWN styles—like they want to—again.

For Sofia Presutti, Joseph and Christian Guzman,
and Baby Hebberd, grand dancers all!
With thanks to Alan Benjamin, at whose suggestion I wrote this text in 1993.
j.n.

For my mom, without whom this book would never have been finished.
d.z.

GINGERBREAD HOUS
602 montauk highwc
westhampton beac
new york 11978 us

SAN: 217-07

Art Direction and Layout by Maria Nicotr

Digital illustrations, rendered from mixed medic

Title font Zothiqu
Text font Century Gothi

Printed in China by Regent Publishing Services Ltc

FIRST EDITION
10 9 8 7 6 5 4 3 2

Library of Congress Cataloging-in-Publication Dat

Nobisso, Josephine
The numbers dance : a counting comedy / by Josephine Nobisso ; illustrated by Dasha Ziborovc
p. cm
Summary: Numerals one through ten divide up by their respective dance styles c
classical, boogie, and western line dancing, until their competition ends in tolerance
ISBN 0-940112-11-6 (hardcover) -- ISBN 0-940112-12-4 (pbk
[1. Dance--Fiction. 2. Stories in rhyme. 3. Counting.] I. Ziborova, Dasha, ill. II. Title
PZ8.3.N715Num 200
[E]--dc2
200500019

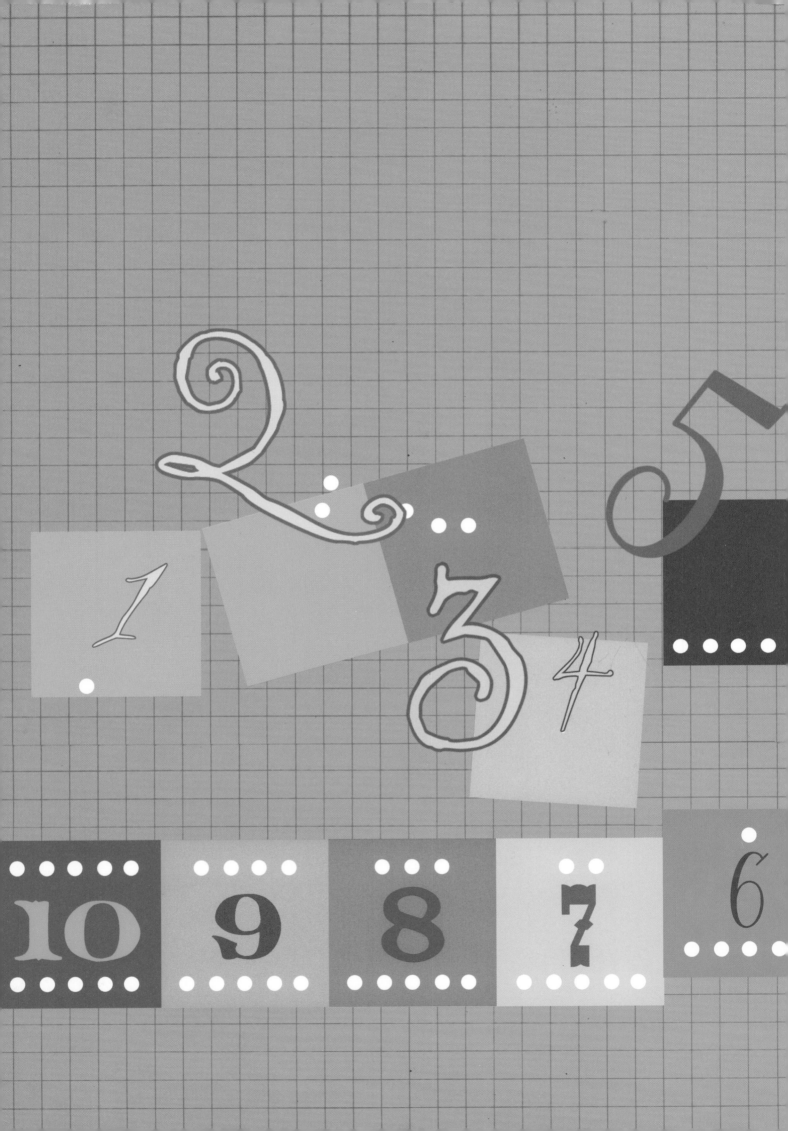